This is dedicated to the

Sheepdog

Past, Present and Future.

Sheepdogs watch over the flock. They keep the sheep safe from danger and protect them from predators. Even though the Sheepdog is there to protect them, sheep generally do not like sheepdogs all that much. The Sheepdog protects the sheep in spite of this. When wolves, bobcats, mountain lions, or thieves come to harm the sheep, the Sheepdog is there to sense danger and alert the Farmer. They bark to alert the Farmer and scare off the threat. If needed they attack. They put themselves in harms way to protect their flock. The Sheepdog does all this for a good meal, a soft bed, a thank you now and again, and the satisfaction of service for others. A quiet professional.

If you help or protect others – You are a Sheepdog!

The Sheepdog

A Children's Book

Written by Rick Yost

Illustrated by Peaks and Pixels

This is a Sheepdog.
His name is Ace.

He is very fast and smart.

Ace's job is to help the Farmer watch over and protect the flock.

He keeps them away from danger and...

...makes sure that they don't wander off.

Ace loves his job.

And he is always on guard to keep the flock safe.

One day while on watch, his nose caught the scent of something that wasn't supposed to be there.

It was a Mountain Lion!

And Mountain Lions are always hungry.

Ace barks ferociously to alert the Farmer and to scare the Mountain Lion away.

He stays between the Mountain Lion and the flock to protect them.

The Mountain Lion decides that he might find an easier meal someplace else.

Ace has done his job, the Farmer is pleased, and the flock is protected.

**But he cannot rest because dangers
and predators are always lurking.**

Ace, the Sheepdog, on duty and always alert.

Be sure to check out the other books
in the Sheepdog Series (Coming Soon).

- Fire Dog
- Police Dog
- Guide dog
- Military dog
- Sled Dog
- Watch dog
- Super hero dog
- Water Dog
- Dog Heroes
- Companion Dog

22505903R00017

Made in the USA
San Bernardino, CA
09 July 2015